MY BEST FRIEND IS A ROBOT

by Elizabeth Traynor

illustrations by
Rose-Ann Tisserand and Greg Huculak

To Eric and Galway

Published by Willowisp Press, Inc.
10100 SBF Drive, Pinellas Park, Florida 34666

Printed in the United States of America

10 9 8 7 6 5 4 3 2 1

ISBN 0-87406-529-1

Contents

1

A STRANGE, GREEN BALL OF LIGHT

It was a dark and stormy morning. I had finished breakfast, and I was sitting in my room before school. The wind moaned. The sky was black and purple. Lightning flashed. Thunder shook our house. It was perfect weather for something weird to happen.

But I didn't care if the weather was terrible. It matched the way I felt. You see, my best friend Ralph moved away to California. I felt rotten. He had only been gone a week, but I really missed him already. We used to do everything together. We were in the same third-grade class, the same Cub Scout pack, and we were on the same baseball team.

We both liked computers, too. Our

favorite computer game was Monster Alert, this great game about space creatures invading the earth. You had to shoot the creatures whenever the computer screen said, "Monster alert!"

But the most fun thing we ever did together was build a robot. Ralph's dad was a computer programmer. He helped us with the robot.

The robot was standing in the corner of my room. He was almost as tall as I was. He was made of metal. There was a little computer inside him. It was connected to my computer so I could program him to walk and talk.

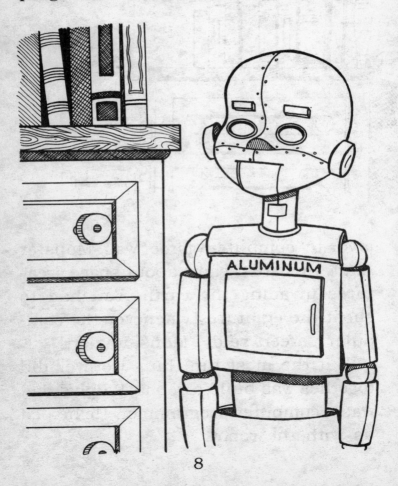

The only problem was that he didn't work. He didn't do anything except stand in the corner of my room. He never moved and he never talked. And without Ralph and his dad, I'd never be able to make the robot work.

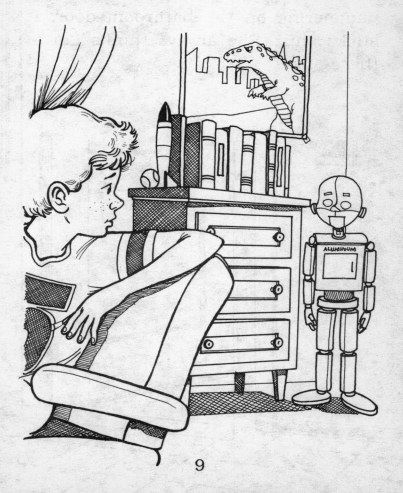

Just then, a loud banging made me leap from my chair. It sounded like a monster was loose in the hall.

"Eric! Get out of the bathroom!" a voice cried. "I have to fix my hair."

It was only my creepy older sister hammering on the bathroom door. It sticks shut. She always thinks I'm in there.

I turned back to my computer and typed out "Hello, computer."

The screen answered, "Hello, dummy." It was a joke Ralph and I had programmed in.

I noticed the sky was getting darker. The wind was moaning past my bedroom window. Big raindrops splattered against the glass. I started to get a little scared. I didn't want the weather to be quite this terrible!

Just then, there was a big crash. I saw a giant ball of strange, green lightning right outside my window! I dove for the floor and hid under my desk!

My computer sputtered! Smoke and sparks shot out from it! The lights went out! Thunder made the house shake and rumble like an earthquake!

Then, from the other side of the room, I heard a voice. A strange, mechanical voice.

It said, "Hello, dummy. Hello, dummy."

2
MONSTER ALERT!

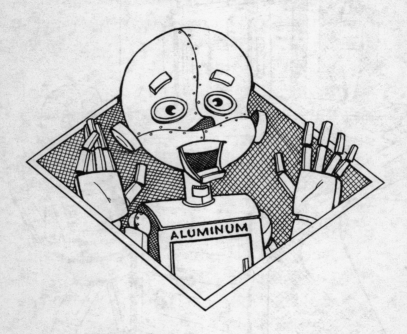

"Augghh!" I screamed. The robot had talked!

"Augghh!" the robot screamed. "Monster alert! Monster alert!"

The lights came back on. I blinked.

Across the room the robot blinked. Slowly, his arms moved to the top of his head. Slowly, he twisted around. Then, he began to stumble around the room. He yelled again, "Monster alert!"

It was the warning from the Monster Alert computer game. When that weird, green light exploded, it must have scrambled his signals.

You could tell he wasn't very good at moving yet. He crashed into the wall and fell over onto his back. His arms and legs wiggled in the air. He looked like a turtle on its back, trying to flip over. I ran to his side and pulled him to his feet.

"Greetings, Master," the robot said. His eyes glowed.

I couldn't believe it. He really worked!

"Just call me Eric," I said.

"Yes, Master," he said. "I'll call you Eric."

Well, maybe he wasn't the smartest robot ever. But he did work. What had

happened? I remembered the glowing green light and the smoke and sparks from the computer. Something had happened to make him start working. But I sure didn't know what!

I heard a knock at the door.

"Eric, are you all right?" my mom

called. "What is all that bumping?"

Uh-oh. How would I explain the robot to her?

"What is that?" the robot asked, staring at the door.

"Shh," I told him. "It's my mother."

"What is mother?" he asked.

"Uh, she's the thing that makes you wash your ears and eat lima beans," I answered.

"Monster alert! Monster alert!" The robot started yelling and running around again.

"Eric! What's going on in there?" Mom asked. "I'm coming in right now!"

The door swung open. "Yeeek!" she shrieked when she saw the robot.

"Yeeek!" the robot shrieked when he saw her.

3

HELLO, DUMMY

I couldn't blame the robot for being scared. My mother is great, but she's really busy, and a little absent-minded. Like last week, she was doing her hair and left this stuff on too long. Now her curly, brown hair is straight and kind of green, like old lettuce.

Before I could explain about the robot,

Mom started talking. "Oh, I'm sorry," she said to the robot. "I didn't know Eric had a friend over before school."

Huh? Couldn't she see this was a robot, not a friend? Then I saw that she wasn't wearing her glasses. They were pushed back into her green hair. Without her glasses, Mom couldn't see very well at all!

"Hello," she said with a smile. "I'm

Eric's mother."

"Hello, dummy," the robot said in a polite voice.

I elbowed him to be quiet. But I don't think my mom heard him, because just

then my bedroom door banged open. It was my sister.

Boy, did she look weird! Her hair was all done up in curlers that looked like rotten worms. There was some shiny, blue mousse on it. And on her face was some gooey mess that glopped down her neck. She looked like a monster that was melting.

And you know what? I wasn't the only one who thought so. The robot made a grinding noise and took off around the room again. "Monster alert! Monster alert!" he cried.

He smashed into the corner of my desk. My marbles spilled out of their jar—all 673 of them! Then the robot slipped on six big blue ones and his feet flew up in the air.

My sister gave me a weird look and shook her head.

"My goodness! Are you hurt?" Mom asked.

"Uh, he's okay, Mom," I answered. I pulled the robot to his feet again. He was heavy! I would have to adjust him so he walked better, or else get stronger

muscles!

"Eric, aren't you going to introduce me to your friend?"

"Uh, sure, Mom. This is...this is..."

I couldn't think of anything to call him. I started to panic. I looked around the room. I looked at the robot. He looked back at me. My goony sister was staring, too.

Then I saw there was something stamped on the robot's chest. It said Aluminum, which was what he was mostly made of.

"Umm, Mom," I said, "Meet my friend, Al. Al U. Minum."

"Hello, dummy," Al said.

4

THAT IS VERY CONFUSING

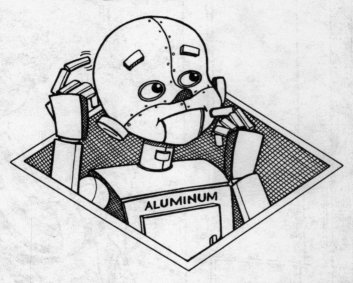

"How nice to meet you, Al," Mom said. "Hmm," she added. "It's getting late. You boys had better get ready for school. The rain has stopped and it's going to be a nice day." Mom left my room smiling. Thank goodness she didn't have her glasses on!

But then my sister looked at me funny and said, "Yes, boys, time to get ready for school." Then she walked out of my room, too. But not before she took another look at Al.

I gulped. My sister didn't need glasses at all. She had very good eyes! Did she know Al wasn't a kid? What if she told Mom?

I don't know why, but I didn't really want Mom to know Al was a robot. Mothers can be a little funny about things sometimes. Maybe she wouldn't want me to have a robot in my room. Especially one that worked.

What could I do with Al while I went to school? Did I dare leave him at home?

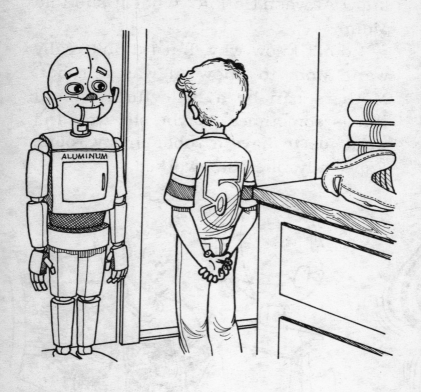

Maybe I could put him in my closet and shut the door.

But when I looked over at Al, he was looking at me. Even though his eyes were just glass lenses, they looked, well, sort of sad. I knew I couldn't make him stay in my closet all day. He would hate that.

I really had no choice. I had to take Al to school with me. I didn't know what would happen when we got there. Would

the other kids know he was a robot? Would the teacher? Taking a robot to school could be a big, big problem!

For one thing, Al was going to have to look a little more like a kid. We were about the same size, so I got out a pair of my jeans and a long-sleeved shirt. I stood back and looked at him.

"Not too bad," I said. But his hair would be a problem. The problem was he didn't have any. I went through my closet and found a wig I had worn last Halloween. Then I put a baseball cap on his head. It was a little weird. But it would have to do.

"Well, Al, I guess we'd better hurry up," I said, putting my old sneakers on his feet. I turned to leave and said, "Shake a leg."

I heard a rattling sound. When I looked over, he was standing on one leg and holding the other, waving it as fast as he could.

"What are you doing?" I asked.

"Shaking a leg, Eric," he answered. "Just like you told me."

"No, Al! That's just an expression," I said. "It means hurry up. You don't really have to shake your leg."

He let go of his leg. Then he said,

"That is confusing, Eric. Very confusing."

It sure was. But why did I feel like
the confusion might get worse? A whole
lot worse.

5

IT ISN'T EASY BEING A ROBOT

When we went downstairs, my sister was looking at herself in the hall mirror. "Don't do that," I said. "You're going to break the mirror."

"Drop dead," she said.

And what do you think happened? Al fell to the floor with a crash. "Like this, Eric?"

"Very funny!" My sister said. "Your friend is a real joker, Eric."

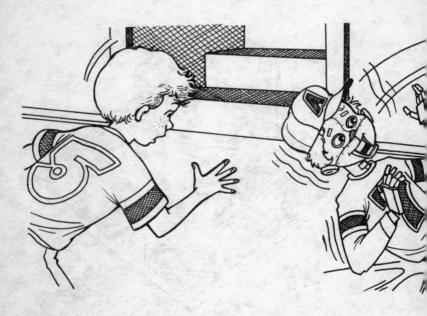

"Get up, Al," I nudged him with my foot. I helped him stand up. "She didn't really mean drop dead. It's just another expression. Sometimes words don't really mean what you think they do."

"Sorry, Eric," Al said. He shook his head. It squeaked a little. "This is all very hard to understand. It isn't easy being a robot."

I thought to myself, it isn't easy being

an inventor either!

I decided to walk to school. After seeing Al walk, I didn't want him to get near a bicycle!

My mom gave me my lunch bag. Then my sister came running up to us. "Here," she said, giggling. "This is Al's lunch," she said. Then she whispered to me, "Don't worry, Eric. I won't tell."

"Why, thank you for making lunch for Eric's friend," said my mom. She still wasn't wearing her glasses.

After Al and I had walked down the block, I opened his lunch bag. In it was a can of oil.

My sister knew that Al was a robot! But she hadn't told Mom! Maybe she

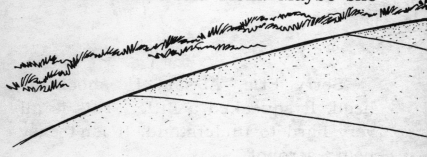

wasn't such a bad sister after all.

When we got to the playground, there were lots of kids. I was pretty nervous. Could I keep Al from doing something weird, like shaking a leg or dropping dead? What would the kids do if they saw that Al was a robot? What would the teacher do?

6
A ROBOT AT SCHOOL

When we got to school, Al and I just hung around at the edge of the playground. Since Ralph moved to California, I didn't have too many friends. I usually just messed around by myself at recess. I usually ate lunch alone. But something happened that morning to change everything.

We were watching some kids play softball. One of the girls hit the ball toward where Al and I were standing. "Heads up, Al," I said, meaning for him to get out of the way of the ball.

I'd forgotten that Al didn't understand all the words we used. So, of course, he put his head straight up in the air. I ducked out of the way. But the ball smacked right onto Al's metal head.

"CLANNGGG!" The ball bounced up. All the kids from the softball game stopped playing and ran over to us.

"Are you all right, Al?" I asked.

"I am just fine, Eric," he answered.
"I put my head up, just like you said."
I didn't even bother to explain to Al

what I really meant. A crowd of kids
had gathered around us. The girl who
hit the ball, said, "That ball hit your
weird friend right on the head and it
didn't even hurt him."

"Yeah," said another kid. "It sounded
like a bell ringing."

"Yeah, well, uh," I said. "My friend
has a hard head."

I didn't know what to do. I was afraid
the kids might find out Al was a robot
and tell the teacher.

Then one of the kids walked up to Al

and knocked on his arm. It sounded just like knocking on a stove pipe. That's because it was a stove pipe!

"Oh, no!" I whispered to Al. "Now

they'll find out for sure. We're in big trouble, Al."

But then a kid named Jason said, "Neat! A real robot! Dressed like a kid!

Where'd you get him, Eric?"

"Well, I, uh, I sort of made him," I answered.

"Awesome!" said another kid.

"Can he talk?" asked Jason.

"I certainly can talk," answered Al.

Well, that just made the kids even more excited. They crowded around me and Al. They shook his hand. They shook my hand. They all wanted to know everything about Al. Jason even taught Al how to give a high five.

"Hello, dummy," Al kept saying. The kids laughed and laughed.

"All right, Al!" Jason said. "You're the coolest dude around!"

Al turned to me. "What does he mean, Eric? I am not cool. It's very warm out here in the sun."

"It's just another expression, Al," I said. He shook his squeaky head.

"Come on, Eric, there's the bell," said Jason. "Is Al coming to class?"

"Uh, yeah, I guess so," I said. "But there's just one thing."

"What's that?" Jason asked.

"Well, I don't want Miss Peters to know that Al is a robot. She might send him home."

Jason put one arm around me and one around Al. "Don't worry, Eric," he said. "We'll do our best to protect Al. Won't we, you guys?"

All the other kids said, "Yeah!"

7

WELCOME TO OUR CLASS

We all filed into the building. It made me feel great to have the kids walking with me and Al. Since Ralph left, I had been feeling pretty lonely.

I held my breath when we walked into the class. Miss Peters was nice. But maybe she'd feel weird about having a robot in her classroom.

Lucky for Al and me, I sat in the back. I headed for my seat and motioned for Al to follow me. Jason nodded his head and walked with Al toward the back. He and a few other kids were huddled around Al so the teacher couldn't see him too well.

Just as Al was about to sit down in an empty desk next to mine, I heard the teacher's voice.

"Oh, Eric," she said. "Is that a new student with you?"

"Uh, yes, Miss Peters," I answered. "His name is Al U. Minum. He's staying at my house. This is his first day in school."

I was glad I didn't have to lie to Miss Peters. It was true. Al was a new student. I just sort of left out the part about him being a metal robot.

Miss Peters looked back in Al's direction. He smiled at her. Then she picked up a book and said, "Welcome to our class, Al. We've got a lot to do today, so we'd better get started right away. Al, can you share Eric's book?"

Al nodded his squeaky head. I decided I had to oil that thing!

Thank goodness Miss Peters was so busy. I don't think she got a very good look at Al. Jason turned around and gave me a thumbs up.

I thought things were going to be okay, until the loudspeaker in the room came on. It was the principal making morning announcements.

The principal's voice over the loudspeaker sounded sort of scratchy and tinny—like Al's voice. When Al heard it,

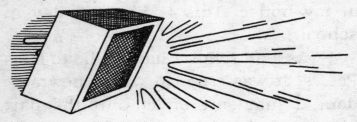

he got all excited.

"Eric! Eric! What is that sound?" he screeched. "Is it another robot?"

"No, Al! Shhh! Don't make so much noise."

"Is it a monster? Is this a monster alert?" he cried.

"No, calm down," I whispered. "It's just the principal making announcements." All I needed was Al running through the halls screaming 'monster alert!'

"Al, remember," I whispered. "There aren't any monsters here in school. And there aren't any other robots either."

"I understand, Eric," Al answered. "No monsters and no other robots."

The principal made a few more announcements. Then he read the menu for lunch, just as he always did.

"For lunch, the cafeteria is serving hot dogs and french fries."

Hot dogs were one of the best lunches at the school. The class cheered. But I heard Al making a weird sound. I looked at him. He looked sick, if a robot can look sick.

"What's wrong?" I asked.

"Did he say we were eating hot dogs?"

"Yeah, but don't worry," I answered. "We brought our lunches from home."

Al had a nervous look on his face. "Do you mean the other students will be eating hot dogs?" he asked.

"That's right," I said.

Al groaned. "The small animals that humans keep as pets? That's terrible to eat them, Eric."

I shook my head. I decided I was going to have to work on Al's circuits. I never knew it was so hard to understand what words really meant!

8

NEW FRIENDS

I was afraid the whole morning that Al was going to start yelling 'monster alert!' or say 'hello, dummy' to Miss Peters, or start shaking his leg, or drop dead on the floor. But he didn't. We did spelling, math, and social studies and the teacher didn't walk back toward us even once.

All the kids in my class helped keep Al's secret. Whenever Miss Peters walked toward the back of the room, someone in the front would ask her a question. When she started to walk to the back closet to get the globe, Jason jumped up and ran to get it for her.

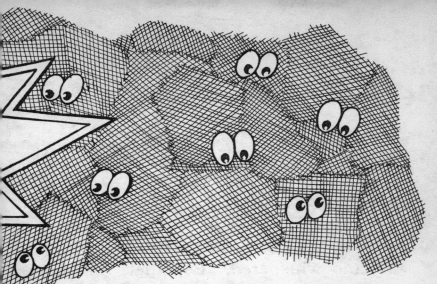

The only close call was when Miss Peters turned out the lights for a science video. It must have reminded Al of the storm earlier in the morning when he came to life.

He started to tremble, which made a loud rattling sound. Then he began to scream "monster alert!" and wave his arms.

It was a lucky thing the lights were out. Miss Peters stopped the video and said, "Stop that shouting, whoever it is! If you can't be quiet, we're going to stop watching the video and work on math problems!"

The class groaned. I leaned over to Al and whispered, "Be quiet, Al! This isn't a monster alert. It's only a science video."

After that, he was quiet. But I was nervous all morning. Keeping an eye on a robot was a big, big job!

When we went out for morning recess, some of the kids started playing softball. I usually just watched them. But this time they asked me and Al to play.

A girl named Stacey loaned Al her baseball glove. First, he put it on his head. But then she showed him how to wear it on his hand and took him out to the field.

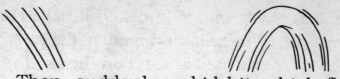

Then, suddenly, a kid hit a high fly ball toward Al. He started to run around under the ball. I could tell he was excited because he kept yelling, "Monster alert! Monster alert!"

"Catch the ball, Al!" I shouted.

He circled around with his arms up in the air as the ball started to come down. I was afraid to look.

The ball came down fast. Even though Al stuck the glove up in the air the way Stacey had shown him, he missed it. It smacked him on the head with a loud clang, just like before.

But this time, it knocked him to the ground. The ball bounced back up in the air. Al wiggled around on the ground, his legs kicking and his arms waving. His lens eyes were looking up at the ball as it came down again.

We all watched as he stuck his ball glove up in the air. We all held our breath. With a loud plop, the ball landed right in the pocket of the glove. A huge cheer went up from all of us kids.

We all ran out to where Al was lying. He held the ball up in the air. He was so excited he kept making funny beeping sounds.

"Great catch, Al!" shouted Jason.

"Are you okay?" I asked.

"Yes, Eric. I am fine," he answered between beeps. "I caught the ball!"

Jason helped me pull Al to his feet. All the kids in my class gathered around me and Al. They pounded me on the back. They exchanged high fives with Al. I could tell I wouldn't feel lonely anymore.

"It's great to have friends, isn't it?"
I whispered to Al as we were walking
back to the building.

"Hello, dummy," Al answered.

About the Author

ELIZABETH TRAYNOR lives on the west coast of Florida with her Irish husband and two sons, Eric, who's in college, and Galway, who's three. A few blocks from their home is a bay where they watch dolphins and manatees play. When she isn't writing books, she likes to make Japanese dolls, write for a Cambodian newsletter, and play with Madcap, the family cat.

She got the idea for Al the robot from being with her son Galway. "Children see life more clearly than adults," explains Elizabeth. "When adults look at things, they see what they expect to see. Kids are different. Besides, I always wanted to have a robot!"

My Best Friend is a Robot is her first book for Willowisp Press.